AND
A CAT
FROM
CARMEL
MARKET

For Karen and Amir, and for Laura, who made it all possible! —A.S.C.

KAR-BEN PUBLISHING®
An imprint of Lerner Publishing Group, Inc.
241 First Avenue North
Minneapolis, MN 55401 USA
Website address: www.karben.com

Main body text set in Calisto MT Std Regular.
Typeface provided by Monotype Typography.

Library of Congress Cataloging-in-Publication Data

Names: Capucilli, Alyssa Satin, 1957– author. | Teplow, Rotem, illustrator.
　Title: And a cat from Carmel Market / Alyssa Satin Capucilli ; illustrated by Rotem
　Teplow.
Description: Minneapolis, MN : Kar-Ben Publishing, [2021] | Audience: Ages 4–8. |
　Summary: After shopping for challah, chicken, and fresh fruit at the Carmel Market
　in Tel Aviv, Bubbe returns home to cook her Shabbat dinner, only to discover that her
　house is filled with unexpected furry guests.
Identifiers: LCCN 2020013134 (print) | LCCN 2020013135 (ebook) |
　ISBN 9781541586703 (library binding) | ISBN 9781541586710 (paperback) |
　ISBN 9781728417639 (ebook)
Subjects: CYAC: Stories in rhyme. | Grandmothers—Fiction. | Cats—Fiction. |
　Grocery shopping—Fiction. | Dinners and dining—Fiction. | Sabbath—Fiction. |
　Sharing—Fiction. | Tel Aviv (Israel)—Fiction. | Israel—Fiction.
Classification: LCC PZ8.3.C1935 An 2021 (print) | LCC PZ8.3.C1935 (ebook) |
　DDC [E]—dc23

LC record available at https://lccn.loc.gov/2020013134
LC ebook record available at https://lccn.loc.gov/2020013135

Manufactured in the United States of America
1-47387-48003-5/8/2020

AND A CAT FROM CARMEL MARKET

Alyssa Satin Capucilli

illustrations by Rotem Teplow

KAR-BEN
PUBLISHING

Bubbe's Shabbat meal was all planned.

She took her list and cart in hand.

"For my Shabbat dinner, I know the place.

. . . I'm off to Carmel Market!"

She chose a challah browned just so,
tall white candles to shine and glow,

a chicken for soup from the butcher shop

. . . and a cat from Carmel Market!

"**Oy!** My cart is growing full,"

Bubbe said with a push and a pull.

"A fine tablecloth is what I need!"

. . . and a cat from Carmel Market!

Bubbe walked from stall to stall.

"These noodles are the best of all.

Potatoes for kugel, carrots, and squash!"

. . . and a cat from Carmel Market!

Then grapes and peaches, plums and pears,
fresh figs and dates beyond compare.

A pomegranate, rosy and ripe

...and a cat from Carmel Market!

"**Oy!** My cart is growing full,"
Bubbe said with a push and a pull.

"A bouquet of flowers is what I need!"

. . . and a cat from Carmel Market!

Bubbe continued on her way.

So many shoppers on this busy day.

"A bit of wine, a brisket to stew . . ."

. . . and a cat from Carmel Market!

In and out and all around,

olives, chickpeas, mint she found.

A babka and a halvah treat

. . . and a cat from Carmel Market!

"**Oy!** My cart is growing full,"
Bubbe said with a push and a pull.

"Some music, I think, is what I need!"

. . . and a cat from Carmel Market!

Bubbe headed home to cook,

with Shabbat groceries from the **shuk**.

"My list is complete. I have it all!"

. . . and a cat from Carmel Market!

She mixed and stirred and tasted with zeal.
She salted and peppered and spiced the meal.

Chicken soup, kugel, roasted meats,
vegetables, fruits, and tasty sweets.

The challah was covered. The guests came in.

With the setting sun came a yowling din!

"Where is it coming from?" they all wanted to know.

. . . from the cats of Carmel Market!

Oy, oy! What should Bubbe do?

Should she send them away or tell them, "**Shoo**"?

Bubbe looked 'round at her table full,
and all she'd brought home with a push and a pull.

But she lit the candles, and what a surprise!

All the cats settled down before her eyes.

"Shabbat shalom to all my friends
. . . and the cats from Carmel Market!"

SOME WORDS TO KNOW

Shuk HaCarmel, or Carmel Market, is a large, bustling market in Tel Aviv. Shoppers flock there daily, but it's especially busy on Fridays when many are there buying food and treats for Shabbat. If you visit, you're sure to see mounds of the freshest fruits, vegetables, spices, and sweets . . . and some cats, too!

Bubbe is the Yiddish word for grandmother.

Shabbat is observed from just before sundown on Friday evening until three stars appear in the sky on Saturday night. Families and friends celebrate at a Friday night meal filled with singing and delicious food. Shabbat candles are lit, and blessings are recited.

Challah is a braided bread eaten on Shabbat and on other Jewish holidays.

Kugel is a pudding dish made from potatoes or noodles.

Babka is a sweet cake often made with chocolate or cinnamon. It's yummy!

Halvah is a type of candy made from flour, tahini, and nuts. You can find it in some American grocery stores and in large "cakes" at a *shuk*, an Arabic word used to describe Israeli marketplaces.

Oy is a Yiddish expression meaning "oh, no!"